Beauty

Andy Warhol

1928–1987

A PENGUIN SINCE 2007

Andy Warhol

Beauty

PENGUIN ARCHIVE

PENGUIN BOOKS

UK | USA | Canada | Ireland | Australia
India | New Zealand | South Africa

Penguin Books is part of the Penguin Random House group of companies
whose addresses can be found at global.penguinrandomhouse.com

Penguin Random House UK,
One Embassy Gardens, 8 Viaduct Gardens, London SW11 7BW

penguin.co.uk

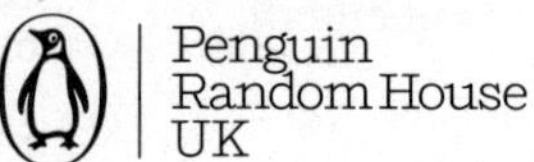

Penguin
Random House
UK

The Philosophy of Andy Warhol first published in the USA
by Harcourt Brace Jovanovich, 1975
First published in Penguin Classics 2007
This selection published in Penguin Classics 2025
005

Set in 11.2/13.75pt Dante MT Std
Typeset by Jouve (UK), Milton Keynes
Printed and bound in Great Britain by Clays Ltd, Elcograf S.p.A.

The authorized representative in the EEA is Penguin Random House Ireland,
Morrison Chambers, 32 Nassau Street, Dublin D02 YH68

A CIP catalogue record for this book is available from the British Library

ISBN: 978–0–241–75232–6

Penguin Random House is committed to a sustainable future
for our business, our readers and our planet. This book is made from
Forest Stewardship Council® certified paper.

Contents

LOVE (SENILITY)

B: *Why didn't you show up last night? You've been in a funny
   mood lately.*
A: *It's just – I can't meet new people. I'm too tired.*
B: *Well, these were old people and you didn't show up. You
   shouldn't watch so much TV.*
A: *Oh I know.*

B: *Is that a female impersonator?*
A: *Of what?*

A: *The most exciting thing is not-doing-it. If you fall in love
   with someone and never do it, it's much more exciting.*

Love affairs get too involved, and they're not really worth it. But if, for some reason, you feel that they are, you should put in exactly as much time and energy as the other person. In other words, 'I'll pay you if you pay me.'

People have so many problems with love, always looking for someone to be their Via Veneto, their soufflé that can't fall. There should be a course in the first grade on love. There should be courses on beauty and love and sex. With love as the biggest course. And they should show the kids, I always think, how to make love and tell and show them once and for all how nothing it is. But they won't do that, because love and sex are business.

But then I think, maybe it works out just as well that nobody takes you out of the dark about it, because if you really knew the whole story, you wouldn't have anything to think about or fantasize about for the rest of your life, and you might go crazy, having nothing to think about, since life is getting longer, anyway, leaving so much time after puberty to have sex in.

I don't remember much about puberty. I probably missed most of it being sick in bed with my Charlie

McCarthy doll, just like I missed *Snow White*. I didn't see *Snow White* until I was forty-five, when I went with Roman Polanski to see it at Lincoln Center. It was probably a good thing that I waited, because I can't imagine how it could ever be more exciting than it was then. Which gave me the idea that instead of telling kids very early about the mechanics and nothingness of sex, maybe it would be better to suddenly and very excitingly reveal the details to them when they're forty. You could be walking down the street with a friend who's just turned forty, spill the birds-and-the-bees beans, wait for the initial shock of learning what-goes-where to die down, and then patiently explain the rest. Then suddenly at forty their life would have new meaning. We should really stay babies for much longer than we do, now that we're living so much longer.

It's the long life-spans that are throwing all the old values and their applications out of whack. When people used to learn about sex at fifteen and die at thirty-five, they obviously were going to have fewer problems than people today who learn about sex at eight or so, I guess, and live to be eighty. That's a long time to play around with the same concept. The same boring concept.

Parents who really love their kids and want them to be bored and discontented for as small a percentage of their lifetimes as possible maybe should go back to not letting them date until as late as possible so they have something to look forward to for a longer time.

Sex is more exciting on the screen and between the pages than between the sheets anyway. Let the kids read about it and look forward to it, and then right before they're going to get the reality, break the news to them that they've already had the most exciting part, that it's behind them already.

Fantasy love is much better than reality love. Never doing it is very exciting. The most exciting attractions are between two opposites that never meet.

I love every 'lib' movement there is, because after the 'lib' the things that were always a mystique become understandable and boring, and then nobody has to feel left out if they're not part of what is happening. For instance, single people looking for husbands and wives used to feel left out because the image marriage had in the old days was so wonderful. Jane Wyatt and Robert Young. Nick and Nora Charles. Ethel and Fred Mertz. Dagwood and Blondie.

Being married looked so wonderful that life didn't seem livable if you weren't lucky enough to have a husband or wife. To the singles, marriage seemed beautiful, the trappings seemed wonderful, and the sex was always implied to be automatically great – no one could ever seem to find words to describe it because 'you had to be there' to know how good it was. It was almost like a conspiracy on the part of the married people not to let it out how it wasn't necessarily completely wonderful to be married and having sex; they could have taken a load off the single people's minds if they'd just been candid.

But it was always a fairly well-kept secret that if you were married to somebody you didn't have enough room in bed and might have to face bad breath in the morning.

There are so many songs about love. But I was thrilled the other day when somebody mailed me the lyrics to a song that was about how he didn't care about anything, and how he didn't care about me. It was very good. He managed to really convey the idea that he really didn't care.

I don't see anything wrong with being alone. It feels great to me. People make a big thing about personal love. It doesn't have to be such a big thing. The same for living – people make a big thing about that too. But personal living and personal loving are the two things the Eastern-type wise men *don't* think about.

I wonder if it's possible to have a love affair that lasts forever. If you're married for thirty years and you're 'cooking breakfast for the one you love' and he walks in, does his heart really skip a beat? I mean if it's just a regular morning. I guess it skips a beat over that breakfast and that's nice, too. It's nice to have a little breakfast made for you.

The biggest price you pay for love is that you have to have somebody around, you can't be on your own, which is always so much better. The biggest disadvantage, of course, is no room in bed. Even a pet cuts into your bed room.

I believe in long engagements. The longer, the better.

Love and sex can go together and sex and unlove can go together and love and unsex can go together. But personal love and personal sex is bad.

You can be just as faithful to a place or a thing as you can to a person. A place can really make your heart skip a beat, especially if you have to take a plane to get there.

Mom always said not to worry about love, but just to be sure to get married. But I always knew that I would never get married, because I don't want any children, I don't want them to have the same problems that I have. I don't think anybody deserves it.

I think a lot about the people who are supposed to not have any problems, who get married and live and die and it's all been wonderful. I don't know anybody like that. They always have some problem, even if it's only that the toilet doesn't flush.

My ideal wife would have a lot of bacon, bring it all home, and have a TV station besides.

I was always fascinated when I watched old war movies where the girls get married by proxy over the phone to husbands across the sea and they'd say, 'I hear you, my darling!' and I always thought how great it would be if they just stayed that way, they'd be so happy. I guess they wanted the monthly check, though.

I have a telephone mate. We've had an on-going relationship over the phone for six years. I live uptown and she lives downtown. It's a wonderful arrangement: we don't have to get each other's bad morning breath, yet we have wonderful breakfasts together every morning like every other happy couple. I'm uptown in the kitchen making myself peppermint tea and a dry, medium-to-dark English muffin with marmalade, and she's downtown waiting for the coffee shop to deliver a light coffee and a toasted roll with honey and butter – heavy on the light, honey, butter, and seeds. We while and talk away the sunny morning hours with the telephone nestled between head and shoulders and we can walk away or even hang up whenever we want to. We don't have to worry about kids, just about extension phones. We have an understanding. She married a staple-gun queen twelve years ago and has been more or less waiting for the annulment to come through ever since, although she tells people who ask that he died in a mudslide.

The symptom of love is when some of the chemicals inside you go bad. So there must be something in love because your chemicals do tell you something.

★

I tried and tried when I was younger to learn something about love, and since it wasn't taught in school I turned to the movies for some clues about what love is and what to do about it. In those days you did learn something about some kind of love from the movies, but it was nothing you could apply with any reasonable results. I mean, the other night I was watching on TV the 1961 version of *Back Street* with John Gavin and Susan Hayward and I was stunned the whole time because all they kept saying was how wonderful every precious moment they had together was, and so every precious moment was a testimonial to every precious moment.

But I always thought that movies could show you so much more about how it really is between people and therefore help all the people who don't understand to know what to do, what some of their options are.

What I was actually trying to do in my early movies was show how people can meet other people and what they can do and what they can say to each other. That was the whole idea: two people getting acquainted. And then when you saw it and you saw the sheer simplicity of it, you learned what it was all about. Those movies showed you how some people act and react with other people. They were like actual sociological 'For instance's. They were like documentaries, and if you thought it could apply to you, it was an example, and if it didn't apply to you, at least it was a documentary, it could apply to somebody you knew and it could clear up some questions you had about them.

In *Tub Girls*, for example, the girls had to take baths with people in tubs, and they learned how to take baths with other people. While we were doing *Tub Girls*. They met in a tub. And the girl would have to carry her tub to the next person she'd have to take a bath with, so she'd put her tub under her arm and carry her tub . . . We used a clear plastic tub.

I never particularly wanted to make simply sex movies. If I had wanted to make a real sex movie I would have filmed a flower giving birth to another flower. And the best love story is just two love-birds in a cage.

The best love is not-to-think-about-it love. Some people can have sex and really let their minds go blank and fill up with the sex; other people can never let their minds go blank and fill up with the sex, so while they're having the sex they're thinking, 'Can this really be me? Am I really doing this? This is very strange. Five minutes ago I wasn't doing this. In a little while I won't be doing it. What would Mom say? How did people ever think of doing this?' So the first type of person – the type that can let their minds go blank and fill up with sex and not-think-about-it – is better off. The other type has to find something else to relax with and get lost in. For me that something else is humor.

Funny people are the only people I ever get really interested in, because as soon as somebody isn't funny, they bore me. But if the big attraction for you is having somebody be funny, you run into a problem, because being funny is not being sexy, so in the end, near the moment of truth, you're not really attracted, you can't really 'do it.'

But I'd rather laugh in bed than do it. Get under the covers and crack jokes, I guess, is the best way. 'How am I doing?' 'Fine, that was very funny.' 'Wow, you were really funny tonight.'

If I went to a lady of the night, I'd probably pay her to tell me jokes.

Sometimes sex doesn't wear off. I've seen cases of couples where the sex for each other didn't wear off over the years.

Couples do become like each other when they're together for a long time, because you like the person and you pick up their mannerisms and their little good habits. And you eat the same food.

Everybody has a different idea of love. One girl I know said, 'I knew he loved me when he didn't come in my mouth.'

Over the years I've been more successful at dealing with love than with jealousy. I get jealousy attacks all the time. I think I may be one of the most jealous people in the world. My right hand is jealous if my left hand is painting a pretty picture. If my left leg is dancing a good step, my right leg gets jealous. The left side of my mouth is jealous when my right side is eating something good. I'm jealous at dinner that somebody else will think of something better to order than I did. I'm jealous of somebody's blurred Instamatics even when I have my own sharp Polaroids of the same scene. Basically, I go crazy when I can't have first choice on absolutely everything. A lot of times I do things I don't want to do at all, just because I'm on stand-by jealousy that somebody else will get to do it instead. As a matter of fact, I'm always trying to buy things and people just because I'm so jealous somebody else might buy them and they might turn out to be good after all. That's one of the stories of my life. And the few times in my life when I've gone on television, I've been so jealous of the host on the show that I haven't been able to talk. As soon as the TV cameras turn on, all I can think is, 'I want my own show . . . I want my own show.'

I get very nervous when I think someone is falling in love with me. Every time I have a 'romance' I'm so nervous I bring the whole office with me. That's usually about five or six people. They all come to pick me up and then we go to pick her up. Love me, love my office.

Everybody winds up kissing the wrong person good-night. One of my ways of thanking the office for coming with me to chaperone is to make myself available to chaperone their dates. One or two of them like to take advantage of that service, because one or two of them are a little like me, they don't want anything to happen. When *I'm* there, they tell me, nothing happens. I make nothing happen. Wherever I go. I can tell when one of them is glad to see me walk in the door, because something's happening and they can't wait for me to make nothing happen. Especially when they're stranded in Italy, because you know how the Italians like to make something happen. I'm the obvious antidote.

People should fall in love with their eyes closed. Just close your eyes. Don't look.

Some people I know spend a lot of time trying to dream up new seductions. I used to think that only the people who didn't work had time to think about those kinds of things but then I realized that most people are using somebody else's time to dream up their new seductions. Most of the people in offices are actually getting paid while they day-dream up their new seductions.

I believe in low lights and trick mirrors. A person is entitled to the lighting they need. Plus, if you learn about sex when you're forty, as suggested earlier, you'd better believe in low lights and trick mirrors.

Love can be bought and sold. One of the older super-stars used to cry every time somebody she loved kicked her out of his loft, and I used to tell her, 'Don't worry. You're going to be very famous someday and you'll be able to buy him.' It worked out just that way and she's very happy now.

Brigitte Bardot was one of the first women to be really modern and treat men like love objects, buying them and discarding them. I like that.

★

The most fashionable girls around town now are the girls of the night. They wear the most fashionable clothes. They were always behind the times, looking old-fashioned, but now they're the first ones on the street with the new clothes. They wised up. More intelligent girls are girls of the night now, too. More liberated. But they all still use those ugly shoulder pocketbooks.

Sex-and-nostalgia is funny to think about. I was walking on the West Side in the Forties, around the honky tonks and I was looking at the 8 x 10 glossies of girls that they put out front. One window-case display had a very 50s look but the pictures weren't yellow with age or anything, so I couldn't tell if those exact girls were inside right then or if that was an old picture left over and the girls inside, instead of being Mamie Van Doren types, were tired ex-hippies. I didn't know. The establishment might have been catering to a crowd who were nostalgic for all the girls they'd tried to pick up in the 50s.

With everything changing so fast, you don't have a chance of finding your fantasy image intact by the time you're ready for it. What about all the little boys who used to have fantasies about girls in beautiful lace bras and silk slips? They don't have a chance of finding what they'd always looked forward to, unless the girl had just made a trip to the local thrift shop, and that's worse than nothing.

*

Fantasy and clothes go together a lot, but the times and mores have thrown that off, too. When clothes-makers were making good clothes out of good materials, an ordinary guy who bought a suit or a shirt without giving too much thought to anything except 'Does it fit?' would be likely to come away with a nice-looking suit with good detailing out of a nice piece of material.

But then labor got expensive and the manufacturers began giving a little less good workmanship for the money every year, and nobody really complained, so they pushed – and they're still pushing to the limit – how little they can give before people will say, 'Is this a shirt?' The moderate-priced clothes-makers really are giving people junk these days. On top of the awful way the clothes are made – long stitches, no linings, no darts, no finished seams – they're made out of synthetics that look awful from the first to the last wearing. (The only good synthetic is nylon, I think.)

No, a person has to be very careful about what he's buying these days or else he'll wind up buying junk. And paying a lot for it too. So this means that *if you see a well-dressed person today, you know that they've thought a lot about their clothes and how they look.* And then that ruins it because you shouldn't really be thinking about how you look so much. The same applies to girls but not as much – they can care a little more about themselves without being unattractively self-interested, because they're naturally prettier. But a man caring about how he looks is usually trying very hard to be attractive, and that's very unattractive in a man.

★

So today, if you see a person who looks like your teenage fantasy walking down the street, it's probably not your fantasy, but someone who had the same fantasy as you and decided instead of getting it or being it, to *look like it*, and so he went to the store and bought the look that you both like. So forget it.

Just think about all the James Deans and what it means.

Truman Capote told me once that certain kinds of sex are total, complete manifestations of nostalgia, and I think that's true. Other kinds of sex have nostalgia in varying degrees, from a little to a lot, but I think it's safe to say that most sex involves some form of nostalgia for something.

Sex is a nostalgia for when you used to want it, sometimes.

Sex is nostalgia for sex.

Some people think violence is sexy, but I could never see that.

'Love' used to have a good number always in Mom's dream book. When I was little Mom used to play the numbers and I remember she used to have a dream book and she'd look up her dream and the book would tell her whether it was a good dream or not, and there were numbers after it which she played. And 'Love' dreams always had a good number.

★

When you want to be like something, it means you really love it. When you want to be like a rock, you really love that rock. I love plastic idols.

People with pretty smiles fascinate me. You have to wonder what makes them smile so pretty.

People look the most kissable when they're not wearing makeup. Marilyn's lips weren't kissable, but they were very photographable.

One of my movies, *Women in Revolt*, was originally entitled *Sex*, I can't now remember why we changed its name. The three female leads were three female impersonators – Candy Darling, Jackie Curtis, and Holly Woodlawn. They played women in varying degrees and various stages of 'liberation.'

Among other things, drag queens are living testimony to the way women used to want to be, the way some people still want them to be, and the way some women still actually want to be. Drags are ambulatory archives of ideal moviestar womanhood. They perform a documentary service, usually consecrating their lives to keeping the glittering alternative alive and available for (not-too-close) inspection.

To get a private room in a hospital you used to have to be very rich but now you can get one if you're a drag queen. If you're a drag queen they want to isolate you from the other patients, but maybe they have enough for a ward now.

I'm fascinated by boys who spend their lives trying to be complete girls, because they have to work so hard – double-time – getting rid of all the tell-tale male signs and drawing in all the female signs. I'm not saying it's the right thing to do, I'm not saying it's a good idea, I'm not saying it's not self-defeating and self-destructive, and I'm not saying it's not possibly the single most absurd thing a man can do with his life. What I'm saying is, it is very hard work. You can't take that away from them. It's hard work to look like the complete opposite of what nature made you and then to be an imitation woman of what was only a fantasy woman in the first place. When they took the movie stars and stuck them in the kitchen, they weren't stars any more – they were just like you and me. Drag queens are reminders that some stars still aren't just like you and me.

For a while we were casting a lot of drag queens in our movies because the real girls we knew couldn't seem to get excited about anything, and the drag queens could get excited about anything. But lately the girls seem to be getting their energy back, so we've been using real ones a lot again.

In *Women in Revolt*, Jackie Curtis ad-libbed one of the best lines of disillusionment with sex when he-as-she, portraying a virgin schoolteacher from Bayonne, New Jersey, was forced to give oral gratification – a blow-job – to Mr America. After gagging and somehow finishing up, poor Jackie can't figure out if she's had sex or not – 'This can't be what millions of girls commit suicide over when their boyfriends leave them . . .' Jackie was acting out the puzzled thoughts so many people have when they realize that sex is hard work just like everything else.

People's fantasies are what give them problems. If you didn't have fantasies you wouldn't have problems because you'd just take whatever was there. But then you wouldn't have romance, because romance is finding your fantasy in people who don't have it. A friend of mine always says, 'Women love me for the man I'm not.'

It's very easy to make *faux pas* when you're talking to a person who's in love, because they're more sensitive about everything. I remember once I was at a dinner party and I was talking to a couple who looked so happy together and I said, 'You are the happiest-looking couple I've ever seen.' That was okay and then I went that little bit further to score my nightly *faux pas*. 'It must have been like a storybook dream love story. I just know you were childhood sweethearts.' And at that point their faces fell and they turned away and avoided me for the rest of the evening. I found out later that they had deserted their husbands and wives and families to go after each other.

So you really have to watch what you say to people about their love lives. When people are in love all their problems are in strange proportions and it's hard to know when you're saying the wrong thing.

★

Andy Warhol

To think about the love problems of people you know is really strange, because their love problems are so different from their life problems.

A drag queen I know is waiting for a real man to fall in love with him/her.
   I always run into strong women who are looking for weak men to dominate them.

I don't know anybody who doesn't have a fantasy. Everybody must have a fantasy.

A movie producer friend of mine hit on something when he said, 'Frigid people can really make out.' He's right: they really can and they really do.

BEAUTY

B: *Does she wear someone's clothes or does she just get them
herself?*

A: *Oh no no no no. She wears her husband's clothes – she goes
to the same tailor. That's what they fight about.*

I've never met a person I couldn't call a beauty.

Every person has beauty at some point in their lifetime. Usually in different degrees. Sometimes they have the looks when they're a baby and they don't have it when they're grown up, but then they could get it back again when they're older. Or they might be fat but have a beautiful face. Or have bow-legs but a beautiful body. Or be the number one female beauty and have no tits. Or be the number one male beauty and have a small you-know-what.

Some people think it's easier for beauties, but actually it can work out a lot of different ways. If you're beautiful you might have a pea-brain. If you're not beautiful you might not have a pea-brain, so it depends on the pea-brain and the beauty. The size of the beauty. And the pea-brain.

I always hear myself saying, 'She's a beauty!' or 'He's a beauty!' or 'What a beauty!' but I never know what I'm talking about. I honestly don't know what beauty is, not to speak of what 'a' beauty is. So that leaves me in a strange position, because I'm noted for how much I talk about 'this one's a beauty' and 'that one's a beauty.' For a year once it was in all the magazines that my next movie was going to be *The Beauties*. The publicity for it was great, but then I could never decide who should be in it. If everybody's not a beauty, then nobody is, so I didn't want to imply that the kids in *The Beauties* were beauties but the kids in my other movies weren't so I had to back out on the basis of the title. It was all wrong.

I really don't care that much about 'Beauties.' What I really like are Talkers. To me, good talkers are beautiful because good talk is what I love. The word itself shows why I like Talkers better than Beauties, why I tape more than I film. It's not 'talkies.' Talk*ers* are *doing* something. Beaut*ies* are *being* something. Which isn't necessarily bad, it's just that I don't know what it is they're being. It's more fun to be with people who are doing things.

When I did my self-portrait, I left all the pimples out because you always should. Pimples are a temporary condition and they don't have anything to do with what you really look like. Always omit the blemishes – they're not part of the good picture you want.

When a person is the beauty of their day, and their looks are really in style, and then the times change and tastes change, and ten years go by, if they keep exactly their same look and don't change anything and if they take care of themselves, they'll still be a beauty.

Schrafft's restaurants were the beauties of their day, and then they tried to keep up with the times and they modified and modified until they lost all their charm and were bought by a big company. But if they could just have kept their same look and style, and held on through the lean years when they weren't in style, today they'd be the best thing around. You have to hang on in periods when your style isn't popular, because if it's good, it'll come back, and you'll be a recognized beauty once again.

Some kind of beauty dwarfs you and makes you feel like an ant next to it. I was once in Mussolini Stadium with all the statues and they were so much bigger than life and I felt just like an ant. I was painting a beauty this afternoon and my paint caught a little bug. I tried to get the paint off the bug and I kept trying until I killed the bug on the beauty's lip. So there was this bug, that could have been a beauty, left on somebody's lip. That's the way I felt in Mussolini Stadium. Like a bug.

Beauties in photographs are different from beauties in person. It must be hard to be a model, because you'd want to be like the photograph of you, and you can't ever look that way. And so you start to copy the photograph. Photographs usually bring in another half-dimension. (Movies bring in another whole dimension. That screen magnetism is something secret – if you could only figure out what it is and how to make it, you'd have a really good product to sell. But you can't even tell if someone

has it until you actually see them up there on the screen.
You have to give screen tests to find out.)

Very few Beauties are Talkers, but there are a few.

Beauty sleep.   Sleeping beauty.
Beauty problems.   Problem beauties.

Even beauties can be unattractive. If you catch a beauty
in the wrong light at the right time, forget it.
I believe in low lights and trick mirrors.
I believe in plastic surgery.

At one time the way my nose looked really bothered
me – it's always red – and I decided that I wanted to have
it sanded. Even the people in my family called me 'Andy
the Red-Nosed Warhola.' I went to see the doctor and
I think he thought he'd humor me, so he sanded it, and
when I walked out of St Luke's Hospital I was the same
underneath, but I had a bandage on.
They don't put you to sleep but they spray frozen
stuff all over your face from a spray can. Then they take
a sandpaperer and spin it around all over your face. It's
very painful afterwards. You stay in for two weeks waiting for the scab to fall off. I did all that and it actually
made my pores bigger. I was really disappointed.
I had another skin problem, too – I lost all my pigment when I was eight years old. Another name people
used to call me was 'Spot.' This is how I think I lost my
pigment: I saw a girl walking down the street and she

was two-toned and I was so fascinated I kept following her. Within two months I was two-toned myself. And I hadn't even known the girl – she was just somebody I saw on the street. I asked a medical student if he thought I caught it just by looking at her. He didn't say anything.

About twenty years ago I went to Georgette Klinger's Skin Clinic and Georgette turned me down. It was before she had a men's department and she discriminated against me.

If people want to spend their whole lives creaming and tweezing and brushing and tilting and gluing, that's really okay too, because it gives them something to do.

Sometimes people having nervous breakdown problems can look very beautiful because they have that fragile something to the way they move or walk. They put out a mood that makes them more beautiful.

People tell me that some beauties lose their looks in bed when they don't do the bed things they're supposed to. I don't believe those things.

When you're interested in somebody, and you think they might be interested in you, you should point out all your beauty problems and defects right away, rather than take a chance they won't notice them. Maybe, say, you have a permanent beauty problem you can't change, such as too-short legs. Just say it. 'My legs, as you've probably noticed, are much too short in proportion to the rest of my body.' Why give the other person the satisfaction of discovering it for themselves? Once it's out in the open, at least you know it will never become an issue later on in the relationship, and if it does, you can always say, 'Well I told you that in the beginning.'

On the other hand, say you have a purely temporary beauty problem – a new pimple, lackluster hair, no-sleep eyes, five extra pounds around the middle. Still, whatever it is, you should point it out. If you don't point it out and say, 'My hair is really dull this time of the month, I'm probably getting my friend,' or 'I put on five pounds eating Russell Stover chocolates over Christmas, but I'm taking it off right away' – if you don't point out these things they might think that your temporary beauty problem is a permanent beauty problem. Why should they think otherwise if you've just met them? Remember, they've never seen you before in their life. So it's up to you to set them straight and get them to use their imagination about what your hair must look like when it's shiny, and what your body must look like when it's not overweight, and what your dress would look like without the grease spot on it. Even explain that you have much better clothes hanging in your closet than the ones you're wearing. If they really do like you for yourself, they'll be willing to use their imagination to think of what you must look like without your temporary beauty problem.

If you're naturally pale, you should put on a lot of blush-on to compensate. But if you've got a big nose, just play it up, and if you have a pimple, put on the pimple cream in a way that will make it really stand out – 'There! I use pimple cream!' There's a difference.

I always think that when people turn around to look at somebody on the street it's probably that they smell an odor from them, and that's what makes them turn around and on.

Diana Vreeland, the editor of *Vogue* for ten years, is one of the most beautiful women in the world because she's not afraid of other people, she does what she wants. Truman Capote brought up something else about her – she's very very clean, and that makes her more beautiful. Maybe it's even the basis of her beauty.

Being clean is so important. Well-groomed people are the real beauties. It doesn't matter what they're wearing or who they're with or how much their jewelry costs or how much their clothes cost or how perfect their makeup is: if they're not clean, they're not beautiful. The most plain or unfashionable person in the world can still be beautiful if they're very well-groomed.

During the 60s a lot of people I knew seemed to think that underarm smell was attractive. They never seemed to be wearing anything washable. Everything always had to be dry-cleaned – the satins, the sewn-on mirrors, the velvets – the problem was that it never was dry-cleaned. And then it got worse when everybody was wearing suedes and leathers, and those *really* never got cleaned. I admit to having worn suede and leather pants myself for a while, but you just never feel clean, and it's degenerate, anyway, to wear animal skins unless it's to keep yourself warm. I'll never understand why they haven't invented something yet that's as warm as fur. So I went back to bluejeans after that degenerate period. Very happily. Bluejeans wind up being the cleanest thing you can wear, because it's just their nature to be washed a lot. And they're so American in essence.

Beauty really has to do with the way a person carries it off. When you see 'beauty,' it has to do with the place, with what they're wearing, what they're standing next to, what closet they're coming down the stairs from.

Jewelry doesn't make a person more beautiful, but it makes a person *feel* more beautiful. If you draped a beautiful person in jewels and beautiful clothes and put them in a beautiful house with beautiful furniture and beautiful paintings, they wouldn't be more beautiful, they'd be the same, but they would *think* they were more beautiful. However, if you took a beautiful person and put them in rags, they'd be ugly. You can always make a person less beautiful.

Beauty in danger becomes more beautiful, but beauty in dirt becomes ugly.

What makes a painting beautiful is the way the paint's put on, but I don't understand how women put on makeup. It gets on your lips, and it's so heavy. Lipstick and makeup and powder and shadow creams. And jewelry. It's all so heavy.

Children are always beautiful. Every kid, up to, say, eight years old always looks good. Even if the kid wears glasses it still looks good. They always have the perfect nose. I've never seen an unattractive baby. Small features and nice skin. This also applies to animals – I've never seen a bad-looking animal. Babies by being beautiful are protected because people want less to hurt them. This applies also to all animals.

Beauty doesn't have anything to do with sex. Beauty has to do with beauty and sex has to do with sex.

If a person isn't generally considered beautiful, they can still be a success if they have a few jokes in their pockets. And a lot of pockets.

Beautiful people are sometimes more prone to keep you waiting than plain people are, because there's a big time differential between beautiful and plain. Also, beauties know that most people will wait for them, so they're not panicked when they're late, so they get even later. But by the time they arrive, they've usually gotten to feel guilty, so then to make up for being late they get really sweet, and being really sweet makes them more beautiful. That's a classic syndrome.

★

I'm always trying to figure out whether if a woman is funny, she can still be beautiful. There are some very attractive comediennes, but if you had to choose between calling them beautiful and calling them funny, you'd call them funny. Sometimes I think that *extreme* beauty must be absolutely humorless. But then I think of Marilyn Monroe and she had the best funny lines. She might have been a lot of fun if she'd found the right comedy niche. We might be laughing at skits on 'The Marilyn Monroe Show' today.

Someone once asked me to state once and for all the most beautiful person I'd ever met. Well, the only people I can ever pick out as unequivocal beauties are from the movies, and then when you meet them, they're not really beauties either, so your standards don't even really exist. In life, the movie stars can't even come up to the standards they set on film.

Some of the very beautiful film stars of the past decades have aged beautifully and some have aged not-so-beautifully, and sometimes you see two stars together today who were once beautiful together in the same movie a long time ago, and now one of them looks and acts like an old woman and the other still looks and acts like a girl. But all of that doesn't matter very much, I think, because history will remember each person only for their beautiful moments on film – the rest is off-the-record.

★

A good plain look is my favorite look. If I didn't want to look so 'bad,' I would want to look 'plain.' That would be my next choice.

I always think about what it means to wear eyeglasses. When you get used to glasses you don't know how far you could really see. I think about all the people before eyeglasses were invented. It must have been weird because everyone was seeing in different ways according to how bad their eyes were. Now, eyeglasses standardize everyone's vision to 20-20. That's an example of everyone becoming more alike. Everyone could be seeing at different levels if it weren't for glasses.

In some circles where very heavy people think they have very heavy brains, words like 'charming' and 'clever' and 'pretty' are all put-downs; all the lighter things in life, which are the most important things, are put down.

Weight isn't important the way the magazines make you think it is. I know a girl who just looks at her face in the medicine cabinet mirror and never looks below her shoulders, and she's four or five hundred pounds but she doesn't see all that, she just sees a beautiful face and therefore she thinks she's a beauty. And therefore I think she's a beauty, too, because I usually accept people on the basis of their self-images, because their self-images have more to do with the way they think than their objective-images do. Maybe she's six hundred pounds, who knows. If she doesn't care, I don't.

But if you do watch your weight, try the Andy Warhol New York City Diet: when I order in a restaurant, I order everything that I don't want, so I have a lot to play around with while everyone else eats. Then, no matter how chic the restaurant is, I insist that the waiter wrap the entire plate up like a to-go order, and after we leave the restaurant I find a little corner outside in the street to leave the plate in, because there are so many people in New York who live in the streets, with everything they own in shopping bags.

So I lose weight and stay trim, and I think that maybe one of those people will find a Grenouille dinner on the window ledge. But then, you never know, maybe they wouldn't like what I ordered as much as I didn't like it, and maybe they'd turn up their noses and look through the garbage for some half-eaten rye bread. You just never know with people. You just never know what they'll like, what you should do for them.

So that's the Andy Warhol New York City Diet.

I know good cooks who'll spend days finding fresh garlic and fresh basil and fresh tarragon, etc., and then use canned tomatoes for the sauce, saying it doesn't matter. But I know it does matter.

Whenever people and civilizations get degenerate and materialistic, they always point at their outward beauty and riches and say that if what they were doing was bad, they wouldn't be doing so well, being so rich and beautiful. People in the Bible did that when they worshiped the Golden Calf, for example, and then the

Greeks when they worshiped the human body. But beauty and riches couldn't have anything to do with how good you are, because think of all the beauties who get cancer. And a lot of murderers are good-looking, so that settles it.

Some people, even intelligent people, say that violence can be beautiful. I can't understand that, because beautiful is some moments, and for me those moments are never violent.

A new idea.
    A new look.
    A new sex.
    A new pair of underwear.

There should be a lot of new girls in town, and there always are.

The red lobster's beauty only comes out when it's dropped into the boiling water . . . and nature changes things and carbon is turned into diamonds and dirt is gold . . . and wearing a ring in your nose is gorgeous.

I can never get over when you're on the beach how beautiful the sand looks and the water washes it away and straightens it up and the trees and the grass all look great. I think having land and not ruining it is the most beautiful art that anybody could ever want to own.

*

The most beautiful thing in Tokyo is McDonald's.

The most beautiful thing in Stockholm is McDonald's.

The most beautiful thing in Florence is McDonald's.

Peking and Moscow don't have anything beautiful yet.

America is really The Beautiful. But it would be more beautiful if everybody had enough money to live.

Beautiful jails for Beautiful People.

Everybody's sense of beauty is different from everybody else's. When I see people dressed in hideous clothes that look all wrong on them, I try to imagine the moment when they were buying them and thought, 'This is great. I like it. I'll take it.' You can't imagine what went off in their heads to make them buy those maroon polyester waffle-iron pants or that acrylic halter top that has 'Miami' written in glitter. You wonder what they rejected as *not* beautiful – an acrylic halter top that had 'Chicago'?

You can never predict what little things in the way somebody looks or talks or acts will set off peculiar emotional reactions in other people. For instance, the other night I was with a lady who suddenly got very intense about a person we both knew and she started to tear apart his looks – his weak arms, his pimply face, his bad posture, his thick eyebrows, his big nose, his bad clothes, and I didn't know what to say because I didn't see why she would be seen with me if she wouldn't be seen with him. After all, I have weak arms, I have pimples, but she didn't seem to notice my problems. I think that some little thing can set off reactions in people, and you don't know what it is in their past that's making them like or not like somebody so much and therefore like or not like everything about them.

Sometimes something can look beautiful just because it's different in some way from the other things around it. One red petunia in a window box will look very beautiful if all the rest of them are white, and vice-versa.

When you're in Sweden and you see beautiful person after beautiful person after beautiful person and you finally don't even turn around to look because you know the next person you see will be just as beautiful as the one you didn't bother to turn around to look at – in a place like that you can get so bored that when you see a person who's not beautiful, they look very beautiful to you because they break the beautiful monotony.

There are three things that always look very beautiful to me: my same good pair of old shoes that don't hurt, my own bedroom, and US Customs on the way back home.

WORK

B: *Hospitals are unbelievable.*
A: *When I was dying I had to write my name on a check.*

Before I was shot, I always thought that I was more half-there than all-there – I always suspected that I was watching TV instead of living life. People sometimes say that the way things happen in the movies is unreal, but actually it's the way things happen to you in life that's unreal. The movies make emotions look so strong and real, whereas when things really do happen to you, it's like watching television – you don't feel anything.

Right when I was being shot and ever since, I knew that I was watching television. The channels switch, but it's all television. When you're really really involved with something, you're usually thinking about something else. When something's happening, you fantasize about other things. When I woke up somewhere – I didn't know it was at the hospital and that Bobby Kennedy had been shot the day after I was – I heard fantasy words about thousands of people being in St Patrick's Cathedral praying and carrying on, and then I heard the word 'Kennedy' and that brought me back to the television world again because then I realized, well, here I was, in pain.

So I was shot at my place of business: Andy Warhol Enterprises. At that point, in 1968, Andy Warhol

Enterprises consisted of a few people who worked for me on a fairly regular basis, a lot of what you might call free-lancers who worked on specific projects, and a lot of 'superstars' or 'hyperstars' or whatever you can call all the people who are very talented, but whose talents are hard to define and almost impossible to market. That was the 'staff' of Andy Warhol Enterprises in those days. An interviewer asked me a lot of questions about how I ran my office and I tried to explain to him that I don't really run it, it runs me. I used a lot of phrases like 'bring home the bacon' so he didn't really understand what I was talking about.

The whole time I was in the hospital, the 'staff' kept on doing things, so I realized I really did have a kinetic business, because it was going on without me. I liked realizing that, because I had by that time decided that 'business' was the best art.

Business art is the step that comes after Art. I started as a commercial artist, and I want to finish as a business artist. After I did the thing called 'art' or whatever it's called, I went into business art. I wanted to be an Art Businessman or a Business Artist. Being good in business is the most fascinating kind of art. During the hippie era people put down the idea of business – they'd say, 'Money is bad,' and 'Working is bad,' but making money is art and working is art and good business is the best art.

In the beginning not everything in Andy Warhol Enterprises was organized too well. We went from art right into business when we made an agreement to provide a certain theater with one movie a week. This made our movie-making commercial, and led us from short movies into long movies into feature movies. We learned a little bit about distribution and soon we started trying to distribute the movies ourselves, but we found out that that was just too hard. I didn't expect the movies we were doing to be commercial. It was enough that the art had gone into the stream of commerce, out into the real world. It was very heady to be able to look and see our movie out there in the real world on a marquee instead of in there in the art world. Business art. Art business. The Business Art Business.

I always like to work on leftovers, doing the leftover things. Things that were discarded, that everybody knew were no good, I always thought had a great potential to be funny. It was like recycling work. I always thought there was a lot of humor in leftovers. When I see an old Esther Williams movie and a hundred girls are jumping off their swings, I think of what the auditions must have been like and about all the takes where maybe one girl didn't have the nerve to jump when she was supposed to, and I think about her left over on the swing. So that take of the scene was a leftover on the editing-room floor – an out-take – and the girl was probably a leftover at that point – she was probably fired – so the whole scene is much funnier than the real scene where everything went right, and the girl who didn't jump is the star of the out-take.

I'm not saying that popular taste is bad so that what's left over from the bad taste is good: I'm saying that what's left over is probably bad, but if you can take it and make it good or at least interesting, then you're not wasting as much as you would otherwise. You're recycling work and you're recycling people, and you're running your business as a by-product of other businesses. Of other *directly competitive* businesses, as a matter of fact. So that's a very economical operating procedure. It's also the funniest operating procedure because, as I said, leftovers are inherently funny.

Living in New York City gives people real incentives to want things that nobody else wants – to want all the leftover things. There are so many people here to compete with that changing your tastes to what other people don't want is your only hope of getting anything. For instance, on beautiful, sunny days in New York, it gets so crowded outside you can't even see Central Park through all the bodies. But very early on Sunday mornings in horrible rainy weather, when no one wants to get up and no one wants to get out even if they *are* up, you can go out and walk all over and have the streets to yourself and it's wonderful.

When we didn't have the money to do feature movies with thousands of cuts and retakes, etc., I tried to simplify the movie-making procedure, so I made movies where we used every foot of film that we shot, because it was cheaper, and easier and funnier. Also so we wouldn't have any leftovers ourselves. Then in 1969 we started editing our movies, but even with our own movies, I still love the leftovers best. The out-takes are all great. I'm scrupulously saving them.

I deviate from my philosophy of using leftovers in two areas: (1) my pet, and (2) my food.

I know I should have gone to the pound for a pet, but instead I bought one. It just happened. I saw him and I fell in love with him and I bought him, so there my emotions made me abandon my style.

I also have to admit that I can't tolerate eating leftovers. Food is my great extravagance. I really spoil myself, but then I try to compensate by scrupulously saving all of my food leftovers and bringing them into the office or leaving them in the street and recycling them there. My conscience won't let me throw anything out, even when I don't want it for myself. As I said, I really spoil myself in the food area, so my leftovers are often grand – my hairdresser's cat eats pâté at least twice a week. The leftovers usually turn out to be meat because I'll buy a huge piece of meat, cook it up for dinner, and then right before it's done I'll break down and have what I wanted for dinner in the first place – bread and jam. I'm only kidding myself when I go through the motions of cooking protein: all I ever really want is *sugar*. The rest is strictly for appearances, i.e., you can't take a princess to dinner and order a cookie for starters, no matter how much you crave one. People expect you to eat protein and you do so they won't talk. (If you decided to be stubborn and ordered the cookie, you'd wind up having to talk about why you want it and your philosophy of eating a cookie for dinner. And that would be too much trouble, so you order lamb and forget about what you really want.)

I did my first tape recording in 1964. I'm trying right now to remember the exact circumstances of what I made my first tape recording of. I remember who it was of, but I can't remember why I was carrying a tape recorder around with me that day or even why I had gone out and bought one. I think it all started because I was trying to do a book. A friend had written me a note saying that everybody we knew was writing a book, so that made me want to keep up and do one too. So I bought that tape recorder and I taped the most interesting person I knew at the time, Ondine, for a whole day. I was curious about all these new people I was meeting who could stay up for weeks at a time without ever going to sleep. I thought, 'These people are so imaginative. I just want to know what they do, why they're so imaginative and creative, talking all the time, always busy, full of energy . . . how come they can stay up so late and not be tired,' and pretty soon it would be four days later. I was determined to stay up all day and all night and tape Ondine, the most talkative and energetic of them all. But somewhere along the line I got tired, so I had to finish taping the rest of the twenty-four hours on a couple of other days. So actually, *A*, my novel, was a fraud, since it was billed as a consecutive twenty-four-hour tape-recorded 'novel,' but it was actually taped on a few separate occasions. I used twenty tapes for it because I was using the small cassettes. And right at that point some kids came by the studio and asked if they could do some work, so I asked them to transcribe and type my novel, and it took them a year and a half to type up one day! That seems incredible to me now because I know that if they'd been any good they could have finished it in a week. I would glance over at them sometimes with admiration because they had me convinced that typing was one of the slowest, most painstaking jobs in the world. Now I realize that what I had were leftover typists, but I didn't know it then. Maybe they just liked being around all the people who hung around at the studio.

Another thing I couldn't understand was all those people who never slept who were always announcing, 'Oh I'm hitting my ninth day and it's glorious!' So I thought, 'Maybe it's time to do a movie about somebody who sleeps all night. But I only had a camera that had three minutes on it, so I had to change the camera every three minutes to shoot three minutes. I slowed down the movie to make up for all the three minutes I lost changing the film, and we ran it at a slower speed to make up for the film I didn't shoot.

I suppose I have a really loose interpretation of 'work,' because I think that just being alive is so much work at something you don't always want to do. Being born is like being kidnapped. And then sold into slavery. People are working every minute. The machinery is always going. Even when you sleep.

The hardest work I ever had to do mentally was go to court and get insulted by a lawyer. You're really on your own when you're up there on the witness stand and your friends can't stand up for you and everything's quiet except for you and the lawyer, and the lawyer's insulting you and you have to let him.

★

I loved working when I worked at commercial art and they told you what to do and how to do it and all you had to do was correct it and they'd say yes or no. The hard thing is when you have to dream up the tasteless things to do on your own. When I think about what sort of person I would most like to have on a retainer, I think it would be a boss. A boss who could tell me what to do, because that makes everything easy when you're working.

Unless you have a job where you have to do what somebody else tells you to do, then the only 'person' qualified to be your boss would be a computer that was programmed especially for you, that would take into consideration all of your finances, prejudices, quirks, idea potential, temper tantrums, talents, personality conflicts, growth rate desired, amount and nature of competition, what you'll eat for breakfast on the day you have to fulfill a contract, who you're jealous of, etc. A lot of people could help me with parts and segments of the business, but only a computer would be totally useful to me.

If I had a good computer I could catch up with my thoughts over the weekend if I ever got behind myself. A computer would be a very qualified boss.

Something I'm not doing these days that I should be doing is meeting more science people. I think that the best dinner party would be where each guest was required to bring a new piece of science news to the dinner table with him. Afterwards, you wouldn't feel you'd wasted any time feeding your machinery with just pieces of food. Nothing about diseases, though. Just pure science news.

People send me so many presents in the mail, but I wish that instead of all the presents and art mailers I would get science mailers in language I could understand. That would make me want to open my mail again.

When I'm working on a business project, I expect bad things to happen all the time. I always expect deals to fall through in the biggest, worst way possible. I guess I shouldn't worry, though. If something's going to happen for you, it will, you can't make it happen. And it never does happen until you're past the point where you care whether it happens or not. An actress friend told me that after she didn't want money any more and after she didn't want jewels any more, that's when she got money and jewels. I guess it's for our own good that it always happens that way, because after you stop wanting things is when having them won't make you go crazy. After you stop wanting them is when you can handle having them. Or before. But never during. If you get things when you really want them, you go crazy. Everything becomes distorted when something you really want is sitting in your lap.

After being alive, the next hardest work is having sex. Of course, for some people it isn't work because they need the exercise and they've got the energy for the sex and the sex gives them even more energy. Some people *get* energy from sex and some people *lose* energy from sex. I have found that it's too much work. But if you have the time for it, and if you need that exercise – then you should do it. But you could really save yourself a lot of trouble either way by first figuring out whether you're an energy-getter or an energy-loser. As I said, I'm an energy-loser. But I can understand it when I see people running around trying to get some.

It's just as much work for an attractive person *not to have* sex as for an *unattractive* person *to have* sex, so it's helpful if the attractive people happen to get energy from sex and if the unattractive people happen to lose energy from sex, because then their wants will fit in with the direction that people are pushing them in.

Along with having sex, being sexed is also hard work. I wonder whether it's harder for (1) a man to be a man, (2) a man to be a woman, (3) a woman to be a woman, or (4) a woman to be a man. I don't really know the answer, but from watching all the different types, I know that the people who think they're working the hardest are the men who are trying to be women. They do double-time. They do all the double things: they think about shaving and not shaving, of primping and not primping, of buying men's clothes and women's clothes. I guess it's interesting to try to be another sex, but it can be exciting to just be your own sex.

A friend really hit it when he said, 'Frigid people really make it.' Frigid people don't have the standard emotional problems that hold so many people back and keep them from making it. When I was in my early twenties and had just gotten out of school, I could see that I wasn't frigid enough to not let problems keep me from working.

I thought that young people had more problems than old people, and I hoped I could last until I was older so I wouldn't have all those problems. Then I looked around and saw that everybody who looked young had young problems and that everybody who looked old had old problems. The 'old' problems to me looked easier to take than the 'young' problems. So I decided to go gray so nobody would know how old I was and I would look younger to them than how old they *thought* I was. I would gain a lot by going gray: (1) I would have old problems, which were easier to take than young problems, (2) everyone would be impressed by how young I looked, and (3) I would be relieved of the responsibility of acting young – I could occasionally lapse into eccentricity or senility and no one would think anything of it because of my gray hair. When you've got gray hair, every move you make seems 'young' and 'spry,' instead of just being normally active. It's like you're getting a new talent. So I dyed my hair gray when I was about twenty-three or twenty-four.

Something that I look for in an associate is a certain amount of misunderstanding of what I'm trying to do. Not a fundamental misunderstanding; just minor misunderstandings here and there. When someone doesn't quite completely understand what you want from them, or when they didn't quite hear what you told them to do, or when the tape is bad, or when their own fantasies start coming through, I often wind up liking what comes out of it all better than I liked my original idea. Then if you take what the first person who misunderstood you did, and you give that to someone else and tell them to make it more like how they know you would want it, that's good, too. If people never misunderstand you, and if they do everything exactly the way you tell them to, they're just transmitters of your ideas, and you get bored with that. But when you work with people who misunderstand you, instead of getting *transmissions* you get *transmutations*, and that's much more interesting in the long run.

I like the people who work for me to have their own ideas about things so they don't bore me, but then I like them to be enough like me to keep me company. I like to be tucked in, but I don't like to be tucked away.

They should have a college course now for maids and call it something glamorous, I think. People don't want to work at something unless there's a glamorous name tagged to it. The idea of America is theoretically so great because we've gotten rid of maids and janitors, but then, somebody still has to do it. I always think that even very intelligent people could get a lot out of being maids because they'd see so many interesting people and be working in the most beautiful houses. I mean, everybody does something for everybody else – your shoemaker does your shoes for you, and you do entertainment for him – it's always an exchange, and if it weren't for the stigma we give certain jobs, the exchange would always be equal. A mother is always doing things for her child, so what's wrong with a person off the street doing things for you? But there'll always be people who don't clean who think they're better than the people who do clean.

I've always thought that the President could do so much here to help change images. If the President would go into a public bathroom in the Capitol, and have the TV cameras film him cleaning the toilets and saying 'Why not? Somebody's got to do it!' then that would do so much for the morale of the people who do the wonderful job of keeping the toilets clean. I mean, it is a wonderful thing that they're doing.

The President has so much good publicity potential that hasn't been exploited. He should just sit down one day and make a list of all the things that people are embarrassed to do that they shouldn't be embarrassed to do, and then do them all on television.

Sometimes B and I fantasize about what I would do if I were President – how I would use my TV time.

Airline stewardesses have the best public image – hostesses in the air. Their work is actually what the waitresses in Bickford's do, plus a few additional duties. I don't want to put down the airline stewardesses, I just want to put up the Bickford ladies. The difference is that airline stewardessing is a New World job that never had to contend with any class stigmas left over from the Old World peasant-aristocracy syndrome.

What's great about this country is that America started the tradition where the richest consumers buy essentially the same things as the poorest. You can be watching TV and see Coca-Cola, and you can know that the President drinks Coke, Liz Taylor drinks Coke, and just think, you can drink Coke, too. A Coke is a Coke and no amount of money can get you a better Coke than the one the bum on the corner is drinking. All the Cokes are the same and all the Cokes are good. Liz Taylor knows it, the President knows it, the bum knows it, and you know it.

In Europe the royalty and the aristocracy used to eat a lot better than the peasants – they weren't eating the same things at all. It was either partridge or porridge, and each class stuck to its own food. But when Queen Elizabeth came here and President Eisenhower bought her a hot dog I'm sure he felt confident that she couldn't have had delivered to Buckingham Palace a better hot dog than that one he bought her for maybe twenty cents at the ballpark. Because there *is* no better hot dog than a ballpark hot dog. Not for a dollar, not for ten dollars, not for a hundred thousand dollars could she get a better hot dog. She could get one for twenty cents and so could anybody else.

Sometimes you fantasize that people who are really up-there and rich and living it up have something you don't have, that their things must be better than your things because they have more money than you. But they drink the same Cokes and eat the same hot dogs and wear the same ILGWU clothes and see the same TV shows and the same movies. Rich people can't see a sillier version of *Truth or Consequences*, or a scarier version of *The Exorcist*. You can get just as revolted as they can – you can have the same nightmares. All of this is really American.

The idea of America is so wonderful because the more equal something is, the more American it is. For instance, a lot of places give you special treatment when you're famous, but that's not really American. The other day something *very* American happened to me. I was going into an auction at Parke-Bernet and they wouldn't let me in because I had my dog with me, so I had to wait in the lobby for the friend I was meeting there to tell him I'd been turned away. And while I was waiting in the lobby I signed autographs. It was a really American situation to be in.

(Also, by the way, the 'special treatment' sometimes works in reverse when you're famous. Sometimes people are mean to me because I'm Andy Warhol.)

Wherever it's possible, you should try to pay people in measurements that are the most suitable for their talent or job. A writer may want to get paid by the word, by the page, by the number of times the reader breaks down crying or bursts out laughing, by the chapter, by the number of new ideas introduced, by the book, or by the year, just to name a few possible categories. A director may want to get paid by the movie or by the foot or by the number of times a Chevrolet appears in the frames.

I'm still thinking about maids. It really has to do with how you're raised. Some people just aren't embarrassed by the idea of somebody else cleaning up after them, and, even though I talk about being a maid not being any different from any other job – because I know it *shouldn't* be considered any different from any other job – still, somehow, deep down, I'm truly embarrassed at the idea of somebody cleaning up after me. If I were really able to think about being a maid the same way I think about, say, being a dentist, I wouldn't be any more embarrassed to let a maid clean up after me than I would be to let a dentist fix my teeth. (Actually, 'dentist' is a bad example, because I *am* embarrassed to let a dentist fix my teeth, especially if my skin is broken out and I'm sitting under those green lights. But I'll stick with that example because the embarrassment I feel about letting someone clean my teeth is nowhere near the embarrassment I feel when someone is around cleaning up after me.)

I confront the problem of how to look at a maid only when I'm staying at a European hotel or when I'm a guest at somebody else's house. It's so awkward when you come face to face with a maid. I've never been able to pull it off. Some people I know are very comfortable looking at maids and even telling them what they'd like done, but I can't handle it. When I go to a hotel, I find myself trying to stay there all day so the maid can't come in. I make a point of it. Because I just don't know where to put my eyes, where to look, what to be doing while they're cleaning. It's actually a lot of work, avoiding the maid, when I think about it.

When I was a child I never had a fantasy about having a maid, what I had a fantasy about having was candy. As I matured that fantasy translated itself into 'make money to have candy,' because as you get older, of course, you get more realistic. Then, after my third nervous breakdown and I still didn't have that extra candy, my career started to pick up, and I started getting more and more candy, and now I have a roomful of candy all in shopping bags. So, as I'm thinking about it now, my success got me a candy room instead of a maid's room. As I said, it all depends on what your fantasies as a kid were, whether you're able to look at a maid or not. Because of what my fantasies were, I'm now a lot more comfortable looking at a Hershey Bar.

It's strange the way having money isn't much. You take three people to a restaurant and you pay three hundred dollars. Okay. Then you take those same three people to a corner shop – shoppe – and get everything there. You got just as filled at the corner shoppe as at the grand restaurant – more, actually – and it cost you only fifteen or twenty dollars, and you had basically the same food.

★

Andy Warhol

I was trying to think the other day about what you do now in America if you want to be successful. Before, you were dependable and wore a good suit. Looking around, I guess that today you have to do all the same things but not wear a good suit. I guess that's all it is. Think rich. Look poor.

TIME

A: *I always think about the people who build buildings and then they're not around any more. Or a movie with a crowd scene and everybody's dead. It's frightening.*

I try to think of what time is and all I can think is . . .

'Time is time was.'

People say 'time on my hands.' Well, I looked at my hands and I saw a lot of lines. And then somebody told me that some people don't have lines. I didn't believe her. We were sitting in a restaurant and she said, 'How can you say that? Look at that waiter over there!' She called him over, 'Honey! Honey? Can you bring me a glass of water?' and when he brought it she grabbed his hand and showed it to me and it had no lines! Just the three main ones. And she said, 'See? I told you. Some people like that waiter have no lines.' And I thought, 'Gee, I wish I was a waiter.'

If the lines on your hands are wrinkles, it must mean your hands worry a lot.

Sometimes you're invited to a big ball and for months you think about how glamorous and exciting it's going to be. Then you fly to Europe and you go to the ball and when you think back on it a couple of months later what you remember is maybe the car ride to the ball, you can't remember the ball at all. Sometimes the little times you don't think are anything while they're happening turn out to be what marks a whole period of your life. I should have been dreaming for months about the car ride to the ball and getting dressed for the car ride, and buying my ticket to Europe so I could take the car ride. Then, who knows, maybe I could have remembered the ball.

Some people decide to be old and then they do exactly what old people are supposed to do. But when they were twenty years old they were doing what twenty-year-olds are supposed to do. And then there are those other people who look twenty all their lives. It's thrilling to see movie stars – since they're more involved in that than most people – who have worked on their beauty, who still have all their energy because they're still working with their young selves.

Since people are going to be living longer and getting older, they'll just have to learn how to be babies longer. I think that's what's happening now. Some kids I know personally are staying babies longer.

I was standing on a street in Paris once and this old lady was looking at me, and I thought, 'Oh she's probably staring at me because she's English,' because English people always know me from a London television disaster that somehow starred me. So I sort of looked away and she said, 'Aren't you Andy?' I said yes and she said, 'You came to my house in Provincetown twenty-eight and a half years ago. You were wearing a sunhat. You don't even remember me, but I'll never forget you in that sunhat. You see, you couldn't take any sun.' I felt so strange because I couldn't remember at all and she remembered to the month. Because to remember 'twenty-eight and a half years ago' without even stopping to calculate must mean that she really kept track and would say, 'Well it's nineteen years now since he was here in the sunhat.' It was very peculiar – her husband was there and they were disagreeing about how long it was. He said, 'No no no. We weren't married yet, remember? So it must have been twenty-six and three-quarter years ago.'

Some people say Paris is more esthetic than New York. Well, in New York you don't have time to have an esthetic because it takes half the day to go downtown and half the day to go uptown.

Then there's time in the street, when you run into somebody you haven't seen in, say, five years, and you play it all on one level. When you see each other and you don't even lose a beat, that's when it's the best. You don't say 'What have you been doing?' – you don't try to catch up. Maybe you mention that you're on your way to 8th Street to get a frozen custard and maybe they mention which movie they're on their way to see, but that's it. Just a casual check-in. Very light, cool, off-hand, very American. Nobody's fazed, nobody's thrown out of time, nobody gets hysterical, nobody loses a beat. That's when it's good. And then when somebody asks you whatever happened to so-and-so you just say, 'Yes, I saw him having a malted on 53rd Street.' Just play it all on one level, like everything was yesterday.

I think I'm missing some chemicals and that's why I have this tendency to be more of a – mama's boy. A – sissy. No, a mama's boy. A 'butterboy.' I think I'm missing some responsibility chemicals and some reproductive chemicals. If I had them I would probably think more about aging the right way and being married four times and having a family – wives and children and dogs. I'm immature, but maybe something could happen to my chemicals and I could get mature. I could start getting wrinkles and stop wearing my wings.

They always say that time changes things, but you actually have to change them yourself.

Sometimes people let the same problem make them miserable for years when they could just say, 'So what.' That's one of my favorite things to say. 'So what.'
  'My mother didn't love me.' So what.
  'My husband won't ball me.' So what.
  'I'm a success but I'm still alone.' So what.
  I don't know how I made it through all the years before I learned how to do that trick. It took a long time for me to learn it, but once you do, you never forget.

★

What makes a person spend time being sad when they could be happy? I was in the Far East and I was walking down a path and there was a big happy party going on, and actually they were burning a person to death. They were having a party and they were happy, singing and dancing.

Then the other day I was on the Bowery and a person in a flophouse jumped out of the window and died, and a crowd went around the body, and then a bum staggered over and said, 'Did you see the comedy across the street?'

I'm not saying you should be happy when a person dies, but just that it's curious to see cases that prove you don't *have* to be sad about it, depending on what you think it means, and what you think about what you think it means.

A person can cry or laugh. Always when you're crying you could be laughing, you have the choice. Crazy people know how to do this best because their minds are loose. So you can take the flexibility your mind is capable of and make it work for you. You decide what you want to do and how you want to spend your time. Remember, though, that I think I'm missing some chemicals, so it's easier for me than for a person who has a lot of responsibility chemicals, but the same principle could still be applied in a lot of instances.

At the end of my time, when I die, I don't want to leave any leftovers. And I don't want to be a leftover. I was watching TV this week and I saw a lady go into a ray machine and disappear. That was wonderful, because matter is energy and she just dispersed. That could be a really American invention, the best American invention – to be able to disappear. I mean, that way they couldn't say you died, they couldn't say you were murdered, they couldn't say you committed suicide over somebody.

The worst thing that could happen to you after the end of your time would be to be embalmed and laid up in a pyramid. I'm repulsed when I think about the Egyptians taking each organ and embalming it separately in its own receptacle. I want my machinery to disappear.

Still, I do really like the idea of people turning into sand or something, so the machinery keeps working after you die. I guess disappearing would be shirking work that your machinery still had left to do. Since I believe in work, I guess I shouldn't think about disappearing when I die. And anyway, it would be very glamorous to be reincarnated as a big ring on Pauline de Rothschild's finger.

I really do live for the future, because when I'm eating a box of candy, I can't wait to taste the last piece. I don't even taste any of the other pieces, I just want to finish and throw the box away and not have to have it on my mind any more.

I would rather either have it now or know I'll never have it so I don't have to think about it.

That's why some days I wish I were very very

old-looking so I wouldn't have to think about getting old-looking.

I really look awful, and I never bother to primp up or try to be appealing because I just don't want anyone to get involved with me. And that's the truth. I play down my good features and play up the bad ones. So I look awful and I wear the wrong pants and the wrong shoes and I come at the wrong time with the wrong friends, and I say the wrong things and I talk to the wrong person, and then *still* sometimes somebody gets interested and I freak out and I wonder, 'What did I do wrong?' So then I go home and try to figure it out. 'Well I must be wearing something that somebody thinks is attractive. I'd better change it. Before things get too far. So I go over to my three-way mirror and I study myself and I see that I have fifteen new pimples on my face and ordinarily that should have stopped them. So I think, 'How weird. I know I look bad. I made myself look especially bad – especially wrong – because I knew a lot of the right people would be there, and still someone somehow got interested . . .' Then I start to panic because I think I don't know what's attractive that I should eliminate before it starts causing me any more trouble. You see, to get to know one more person is just too hard, because each new person takes up more time and space. The way to keep some of your time to yourself is to maintain yourself so unattractively that nobody else is interested in any of it.

★

I look at professional people like comedians in nightclubs, and I'm always impressed with their perfect timing, but I could never understand how they can bear to say exactly the same thing all the time. Then I realized what's the difference, because you're always repeating your same things all the time anyway, whether or not somebody asks you or it's your job. You're usually making the same mistakes. You apply your usual mistakes to every new category or field you go into.

Whenever I'm interested in something, I know the timing's off, because I'm always interested in the right thing at the wrong time. I should just be getting interested after I'm not interested any more, because right after I'm embarrassed to still be thinking about a certain idea, that's when the idea is just about to make somebody a few million dollars. My same good mistakes.

I learned something about time when I used to have to go around New York and see people by appointment in their offices. Somebody would give me an appointment at ten o'clock, so I'd beat my brains out to get there at exactly ten, and I would get there and they wouldn't see me until five minutes to one. So when you go through this a hundred times and you hear, 'Ten o'clock?' you say, 'Weeeellll, that sounds funny, I think I'll show up at five minutes to one.' So I used to show up at five minutes to one and it always worked. That's when I would see the person. So I learned. It was like being a laboratory rat and they put you through all those tests and you get rewarded when you do it right, and when you do it wrong you're kicked back, so you learn. So I learned when people would be around.

The only time my system didn't work was with Liz Taylor. I was in Rome appearing in a movie with her and for a week every day she was hours late for shooting, and finally I thought, 'Well listen, let's just take our time tomorrow and not get up at six-thirty.' So that day she got there before everybody else. She was there before the wardrobe lady and the key grip. She practically had the coffee perking. She really keeps you on your toes. She did the same thing I did, in reverse, and I was thrown off because I didn't know her well enough to predict her. Liz Taylor, in being late fifty times and then early once, must be applying the same principle that I do by having my hair gray so when I do something with a normal amount of energy it seems 'young.' Liz Taylor when she's on time seems 'early.' It's like you get a new talent all of a sudden by being so bad at something for so long, and then suddenly one day being not quite so bad.

I like the idea that people in New York now have to wait in line for movies. You go by so many theaters where there are long, long lines. But nobody looks unhappy about it. It costs so much money just to live now, and if you're on a date, you can spend your whole date time in line, and that way it saves you money because you don't have to think of other things to do while you're waiting and you get to know your person, and you suffer a little together, and then you're entertained for two hours. So you've gotten very close, you've shared a complete experience. And the idea of waiting for something makes it more exciting anyway. Never getting in is the most exciting, but after that waiting to get in is the most exciting.

If I only had time for one vacation every ten years I still don't think I'd want to go anywhere. I'd probably just go to my room, fluff up the pillow, turn on a couple of TVs, open a box of Ritz crackers, break the seal on a box of Russell Stovers, sit down with the latest issue of every magazine except *TV Guide* from the corner newsstand, then pick up the phone and call everybody I know to ask them to look in their *TV Guides* to tell me what's on, what's been on, what's going to be on. I also enjoy rereading the newspaper. Especially in Paris. I can't reread the international *Herald Tribune* enough when I'm in Paris. I love to while away the hours while other people do their meanwhiles, as long as they call in to report. In my room, time moves so slowly for me, it's only outside that everything is happening so fast.

I don't like to travel, because I really like slow time and for a plane you have to leave three or four hours ahead of time, so that's a day right there. If you really want your life to pass like a movie in front of you, just travel, you can forget your life.

★

I like a rut. People call me up and say, 'I hope I'm not disturbing your rut, calling you up like this.' They know how much I like it.

One mistake I make time after time is not following the Golden Rule: I hold elevators. Also, even though I try to throw things away and simplify my life, I palm things off on other people.

What makes a movie fast is when you see it, and then when you see it a second time it goes really fast. If you really want to suffer, go see something and then go see it again. You'll see that your suffering goes by quicker the second time.

I can see a murder mystery one night, and then see it a second time the next night and still not know who did it until the very last minute. So I know there's something *really wrong* with me. I mean, if I can sit there and watch another *Thin Man* and watch it again the next night, and still not know who the murderer is again until the very last minute . . . And I'll be just as curious and just as on-the-edge-of-my-chair waiting to find out, and just as shocked as I was the night before. If I've seen it fifteen times, then *maybe* one time out of the fifteen it'll come back to me and I might get a glimmer of who did it. I guess time is actually the best plot – the suspense of seeing if you'll remember.

Digital clocks and watches really show me that there's a new time on my hand. And it's sort of frightening.

Andy Warhol

Somebody has thought of a new way to show time, so I guess we won't be saying one 'o'clock' too much longer, because that's 'of the clock' or 'by the clock' and there won't be any more clocks: it'll be 'one time' instead of 'one o'clock' and 'three-thirty time' and 'four-forty-five time.'

When I was little and I was sick a lot, those sick times were like little intermissions. Innermissions. Playing with dolls.

I never used to cut out my cut-out dolls. Some people who've worked with me might suggest that I had someone else cut them out for me, but really the reason I didn't cut them out was that I didn't want to ruin the nice pages they were on. I always left my cut-out dolls in my cut-out books.

About Time

> From time to time
> Do time
> Time yourself
>
> weekends.
>
> In time
> In no time
> In good time
> Between time
> Time and again

Lifetime
Time-worn

Pass time
Mark time
Buy time
Keep time

On time
In time
Time off
Time out
Time in
Time card
Time lapse
Time zone

The beforetime
The meantime
The aftertime
The All-time –

When I look around today, the biggest anachronism I see is pregnancy. I just can't believe that people are still pregnant.

The best time for me is when I don't have any problems that I can't buy my way out of.

ATMOSPHERE

B: *I wanted to make a film that showed how sad and lyrical
it is for those two old ladies to be living in those rooms full
of newspapers and cats.*
A: *You shouldn't make it sad. You should just say, 'This is how
people today are doing things.'*

Space is all one space and thought is all one thought, but my mind divides its spaces into spaces into spaces and thoughts into thoughts into thoughts. Like a large condominium. Occasionally I think about the one Space and the one Thought, but usually I don't. Usually I think about my condominium.

The condominium has hot and cold running water, a few Heinz pickles thrown in, some chocolate-covered cherries, and when the Woolworth's hot fudge sundae switch goes on, then I know I really have something.

(This condominium meditates a lot: it's usually closed for the afternoon, evening, and morning.)

Your mind makes spaces into spaces. It's a lot of hard work. A lot of hard spaces. As you get older you get more spaces, and more compartments. And more things to put in the compartments.

To be really rich, I believe, is to have one space. One big empty space.

I really believe in empty spaces, although, as an artist, I make a lot of junk.

Empty space is never-wasted space.

Wasted space is any space that has art in it.

*

An artist is somebody who produces things that people don't need to have but that he – for *some reason* – thinks it would be a good idea to give them.

Business Art is a much better thing to be making than Art Art, because Art Art doesn't support the space it takes up, whereas Business Art does. (If Business Art doesn't support its own space it goes out-of-business.)

So on the one hand I really believe in empty spaces, but on the other hand, because I'm still making some art, I'm still making junk for people to put in their spaces that I believe should be empty: i.e., I'm helping people *waste* their space when what I really want to do is help them *empty* their space.

I go even further in not following my own philosophy, because I can't even empty my own spaces. It's not that my philosophy is failing me, it's that I am failing my own philosophy. I breach what I preach more than I practice it.

When I look at things, I always see the space they occupy. I always want the space to reappear, to make a comeback, because it's lost space when there's something in it. If I see a chair in a beautiful space, no matter how beautiful the chair is, it can never be as beautiful to me as the plain space.

My favorite piece of sculpture is a solid wall with a hole in it to frame the space on the other side.

★

I believe that everyone should live in one big empty space. It can be a small space, as long as it's clean and empty. I like the Japanese way of rolling everything up and locking it away in cupboards. But I wouldn't even have the cupboards, because that's hypocritical. But if you can't go all the way and you really feel you need a closet, then your closet should be a totally separate piece of space so you don't use it as a crutch too much. If you live in New York, your closet should be, at the very least, in New Jersey. Aside from false dependency, another reason for keeping your closet at a good distance from where you live is that you don't want to feel you're living next door to your own dump. Another person's dump wouldn't bother you so much because you wouldn't know exactly what was in it, but thinking about your own closet, and knowing every little thing that's in it, could drive you crazy.

Everything in your closet should have an expiration date on it the way milk and bread and magazines and newspapers do, and once something passes its expiration date, you should throw it out.

What you should do is get a box for a month, and drop everything in it and at the end of the month lock it up. Then date it and send it over to Jersey. You should try to keep track of it, but if you can't and you lose it, that's fine, because it's one less thing to think about, another load off your mind.

Tennessee Williams saves everything up in a trunk and then sends it out to a storage place. I started off myself with trunks and the odd pieces of furniture, but then I went around shopping for something better and now I just drop everything into the same-size brown cardboard boxes that have a color patch on the side for the month of the year. I really hate nostalgia, though, so deep down I hope they all get lost and I never have to look at them again. That's another conflict. I want to throw things right out the window as they're handed to me, but instead I say thank you and drop them into the box-of-the-month. But my other outlook is that I really do want to save things so they can be used again someday.

There should be supermarkets that sell things and supermarkets that buy things back, and until that equalizes, there'll be more waste than there should be. Everybody would always have something to sell back, so everybody would have money, because everybody would have something to sell. We all have something, but most of what we have isn't salable, there's such a preference today for brand new things. People should be able to sell their old cans, their old chicken bones, their old shampoo bottles, their old magazines. We have to get more organized. People who tell you we're running out of things are just making the prices go up higher. How can we be running out of anything when there's always, if I'm not mistaken, the same amount of matter in the Universe, with the exception of what goes into the black holes?

I think about people eating and going to the bathroom all the time, and I wonder why they don't have a tube up their behind that takes all the stuff they eat and recycles it back into their mouth, regenerating it, and then they'd never have to think about buying food or eating it. And they wouldn't even have to see it – it wouldn't even be dirty. If they wanted to, they could artificially color it on the way back in. Pink. (I got the idea from thinking that bees shit honey, but then I found out that honey isn't bee-shit, it's bee regurgitation, so the honeycombs aren't bee bathrooms as I had previously thought. The bees therefore must run off somewhere else to do it.)

Free countries are great, because you can actually sit in somebody else's space for a while and pretend you're a part of it. You can sit in the Plaza Hotel and you don't even have to live there. You can just sit and watch the people go by.

There are different ways for individual people to take over space – to command space. Very shy people don't even want to take up the space that their body actually takes up, whereas very outgoing people want to take up as much space as they can get.

Before media there used to be a physical limit on how much space one person could take up by themselves. People, I think, are the only things that know how to take up more space than the space they're actually in, because with media you can sit back and still let yourself fill up space on records, in the movies, most exclusively on the telephone and least exclusively on television.

Some people must go crazy when they realize how

much space they've managed to command. If you were the star of the biggest show on television and took a walk down an average American street one night while you were on the air, and if you looked through windows and saw yourself on television in everybody's living room, taking up some of their space, can you imagine how you would feel?

I don't think anybody, no matter how famous they are in other fields, could ever feel as peculiar as a television star. Not even the biggest rock star whose records are playing on sound systems everywhere he goes could feel as peculiar as someone who knows he's on everybody's television regularly. No matter how small he is, he has all the space anyone could ever want, right there in the television box.

You should have contact with your closest friends through the most intimate and exclusive of all media – the telephone.

I've always had a conflict because I'm shy and yet I like to take up a lot of personal space. Mom always said, 'Don't be pushy, but let everybody know you're around.' I wanted to command more space than I was commanding, but then I knew I was too shy to know what to do with the attention if I did manage to get it. That's why I love television. That's why I feel that television is the media I'd most like to shine in. I'm really jealous of everybody who's got their own show on television.

As I said, I want a show of my own – called *Nothing Special*.

I'm impressed with people who can create new spaces with the right words. I only know one language, and sometimes in the middle of a sentence I feel like a foreigner trying to talk it because I have word spasms where the parts of some words begin to sound peculiar to me and in the middle of saying the word I'll think, 'Oh, this can't be right – this sounds very peculiar, I don't know if I should try to finish up this word or try to make it into something else, because if it comes out good it'll be right, but if it comes out bad it'll sound retarded,' and so in the middle of words that are over one syllable, I sometimes get confused and try to graft other words on top of them. Sometimes this makes good journalism and when they quote me it looks good in print, and other times it's very embarrassing. You can never predict what will come out when the words you're saying start to sound strange to you and you start to patch.

I really love English – like I love everything else that's American – it's just that I don't do that well with it. My hairdresser keeps telling me that learning foreign languages is good for business (he knows five, but then the little kids in Europe giggle when he talks, so I don't know how well he really knows them) and he tells me I should learn at least one, but I just can't. I can hardly talk what I already talk, so I don't want to branch out.

I admire people who do well with words, though, and I thought Truman Capote filled up space with words so well that when I first got to New York I began writing short fan letters to him and calling him on the phone every day until his mother told me to quit it.

I think a lot about 'space writers' – the writers who get paid by how much they write. I always think quantity is the best gauge on anything (because you're always doing the same thing, even if it looks like you're doing something else), so I set my sights on becoming a 'space artist.' When Picasso died I read in a magazine that he had made four thousand masterpieces in his lifetime and I thought, 'Gee, I could do that in a day.' So I started. And then I found out, 'Gee, it takes more than a day to do four thousand pictures.' You see, the way I do them, with my technique, I really thought I could do four thousand in a day. And they'd all be masterpieces because they'd all be the same painting. And I started and I got up to about five hundred and then I stopped. But it took more than a day, I think it took a month. So at five hundred a month, it would have taken me about eight months to do four thousand masterpieces – to be a 'space artist' and fill up spaces that I don't believe should be filled up anyway. It was disillusioning for me, to realize it would take me that long.

I like painting on a square because you don't have to decide whether it should be longer-longer or shorter-shorter or longer-shorter: it's just a square. I always wanted to do nothing but the same-size picture, but then somebody always comes along and says, 'You have to do it a little bit bigger,' or 'A little bit smaller.' You see,

I think every painting should be the same size and the same color so they're all interchangeable and nobody thinks they have a better painting or a worse painting. And if the one 'master painting' is good, they're all good. Besides, even when the subject is different, people always paint the same painting.

When I have to think about it, I know the picture is wrong. And sizing is a form of thinking, and coloring is too. My instinct about painting says, 'If you don't think about it, it's right.' As soon as you have to decide and choose, it's wrong. And the more you decide about, the more wrong it gets. Some people, they paint abstract, so they sit there thinking about it because their thinking makes them feel they're doing something. But my thinking never makes me feel I'm doing anything. Leonardo da Vinci used to convince his patrons that his thinking time was worth something – worth even more than his painting time – and that may have been true for him, but I know that my thinking time isn't worth anything. I only expect to get paid for my 'doing' time.

When I paint:

I look at my canvas and I space it out right. I think, 'Well, over here in this corner it looks like it sort of belongs,' and so I say, 'Oh yes, that's where it belongs, all right.' So I look at it again and I say, 'The space in that corner there needs a little blue,' and so I put my blue up there and then, then I look over there and it looks blue over there so I take my brush and I move it over there and I make it blue over there, too. And then it needs to be more spaced, so I take my little blue brush and I blue it over there, and then I take my green brush and I put my green brush on it and I green it there, and then I walk back and I look at it and see if it's spaced right. And then – sometimes it's not spaced right – I take my colors and I put another little green over there and then if it's spaced right I leave it alone.

Usually, all I need is tracing paper and a good light. I can't understand why I was never an abstract expressionist, because with my shaking hand I would have been a natural.

I got a little into technology a couple of times. One of the times was when I thought it was the end of my art. I thought I was really really finished, so to mark the end of my art career I made silver pillows that you could just fill up with balloons and let fly away. I made them for a performance of the Merce Cunningham Dance Company. And then it turned out they didn't float away and we were stuck with them, so I guessed I wasn't really finished with art, since there I was, back again, putting anchors on the pillows. I had actually announced I was retiring from art. But then the Silver Space Pillows didn't float away and my career didn't float away, either. Incidentally, I've always said that silver was my favorite color because it reminded me of space, but now I'm thinking that over.

Another way to take up more space is with perfume.

I really love wearing perfume.

I'm not exactly a snob about the bottle a cologne comes in, but I am impressed with a good-looking presentation. It gives you confidence when you're picking up a well-designed bottle.

People have told me that the lighter your skin, the lighter the color perfume you should use. And vice-versa. But I can't limit myself to one range. (Besides, I'm sure hormones have a lot to do with how a perfume smells on your skin – I'm sure the right hormones can make Chanel No. 5 smell very butch.)

I switch perfumes all the time. If I've been wearing one perfume for three months, I force myself to give it up, even if I still feel like wearing it, so whenever I smell it again it will always remind me of those three months. I never go back to wearing it again; it becomes part of my permanent smell collection.

Sometimes at parties I slip away to the bathroom just to see what colognes they've got. I never look at anything else – I don't snoop – but I'm compulsive about seeing if there's some obscure perfume I haven't tried yet, or a good old favorite I haven't smelled in a long time. If I see something interesting, I can't stop myself from pouring it on. But then for the rest of the evening, I'm paranoid that the host or hostess will get a whiff of me and notice that I smell like somebody-they-know.

Of the five senses, smell has the closest thing to the full power of the past. Smell really is transporting. Seeing, hearing, touching, tasting are just not as powerful as smelling if you want your whole being to go back for a second to something. Usually I don't want to, but by having smells stopped up in bottles, I can be in control and can only smell the smells I want to, when I want to, to get the memories I'm in the mood to have. Just for a second. The good thing about a smell-memory is that the feeling of being transported stops the instant you stop smelling, so there are no aftereffects. It's a neat way to reminisce.

My collection of semi-used perfumes is very big by now, although I didn't start wearing lots of them until the early 60s. Before that the smells in my life were all just whatever happened to hit my nose by chance. But then I realized I had to have a kind of smell museum so certain smells wouldn't get lost forever. I loved the way the lobby of the Paramount Theater on Broadway used to smell. I would close my eyes and breathe deep whenever I was in it. Then they tore it down. I can look all I want at a picture of that lobby, but so what? I can't ever smell it again. Sometimes I picture a botany book in the future saying something like, 'The lilac is now extinct. Its fragrance is thought to have been simi-lar to – ?' and then what can they say? Maybe they'll be able to give it as a chemical formula. Maybe they already can.

I used to be afraid I would eventually run through and use up all the good colognes and there'd be nothing left but things like 'Grape' and 'Musk.' But now that I've been to the *profumerias* of Europe and seen all the colognes and perfumes they have there, I don't worry any more.

I get very excited when I read advertisements for

perfume in the fashion magazines that were published in the 30s and 40s. I try to imagine from their names what they smelled like and I go crazy because I want to smell them all so much:

Guerlain's: 'Sous le Vent'
Lucien Le Long's: 'Jabot,' 'Gardénia,' 'Mon Image,'
    'Opening Night'
Prince Matchabelli's: 'Princess of Wales' in memory
    of Alexandra
Ciro's: 'Surrender,' 'Réflexions'
Lenthéric's: 'A Bientôt,' 'Shanghai,' 'Gardénia de
    Tahiti'
Worth's: 'Imprudence'
Marcel Rochas': 'Avenue Matignon,' 'Air Jeune'
D'Orsay's: 'Trophée,' 'Le Dandy,' 'Toujours
    Fidèle,' 'Belle de Jour'
Coty's: 'A Suma,' 'La Fougeraie au Crépuscule'
    (Fernery at Twilight)
Corday's: 'Tzigane,' 'Possession,' 'Orchidée Bleue,'
    'Voyage à Paris'
Chanel's: brisk 'Cuir de Russie' (Russian Leather);
    romantic 'Glamour'; melting 'Jasmine'; tender
    'Gardénia'
Molinelle's: 'Venez Voir'
Houbigant's: 'Countryclub,' 'Demi-Jour' (Twilight)
Bonwit Teller's: '721'
Helena Rubinstein's: 'Town,' 'Country'
Weil's: Eau de Cologne 'Carbonique'
Kathleen Mary Quinlan's: 'Rhythm'

Lengyel's (pronounced 'len-jel'): 'Impériale Russe'
Chevalier Garde's: 'H.R.R.,' 'Fleur de Perse,' 'Roi
    de Rome'
Saravel's: 'White Christmas'

When I'm walking around New York I'm always aware of the smells around me: the rubber mats in office buildings; upholstered seats in movie theaters; pizza; Orange Julius; espresso-garlic-oregano; burgers; dry cotton tee-shirts; neighborhood grocery stores; chic grocery stores; the hot dogs and sauerkraut carts; hardware store smell; stationery store smell; souvlaki; the leather and rugs at Dunhill, Mark Cross, Gucci; the Moroccan-tanned leather on the street-racks; new magazines, back-issue magazines; typewriter stores; Chinese import stores (the mildew from the freighter); India import stores; Japanese import stores; record stores; health food stores; soda-fountain drugstores; cut-rate drugstores; barber shops; beauty parlors; delicatessens; lumber yards; the wood chairs and tables in the NY Public Library; the donuts, pretzels, gum, and grape soda in the subways; kitchen appliance departments; photo labs; shoe stores; bicycle stores; the paper and printing inks in Scribner's, Brentano's, Doubleday's, Rizzoli, Marboro, Bookmasters, Barnes & Noble; shoe-shine stands; grease-batter; hair pomade; the good cheap candy smell in the front of Woolworth's and the dry-goods smell in the back; the horses by the Plaza Hotel; bus and truck exhaust; architects' blueprints; cumin, fenugreek, soy sauce, cinnamon; fried platanos; the train tracks in Grand Central Station; the banana smell of dry cleaners; exhausts from apartment house laundry rooms; East Side bars (creams); West Side bars (sweat); newspaper stands; record stores; fruit stands in all the different seasons – strawberry, watermelon, plum, peach, kiwi, cherry, Concord grape, tangerine, murcot, pineapple, apple – and I love the way the smell of each fruit gets into the rough wood of the crates and into the tissue-paper wrappings.

I know from experience that I prefer city space to country space. I love the idea of being in the country, but then when I get there it comes back to me that:

> I love to walk but I can't
> I love to swim but I can't
> I love to sit in the sun but I can't
> I love to smell the flowers but I can't
> I love to play tennis but I can't
> I love to water-ski but I can't

The list could run longer, but that's the idea, and the reason 'I can't' is simply because I'm *not the type*. You just can't do things that you're not the type to do. You can *say things* that you're not the type to say, but you can't *do things* that you're not the type to do. It's a bad idea.

Also, when I'm in the country, I love to watch television but I can't, because the reception is usually too bad.

(By the way, people will often try to convince you to do something by saying that it doesn't matter if you're not the type, or that you could be the type if you wanted to be, but don't break down and try to do something that you're not the type to do, because you know what type you are, nobody else does.)

I'm a city boy. In the big cities they've set it up so you can go to a park and be in a miniature countryside, but in the countryside they don't have any patches of big city, so I get very homesick.

Another reason I like the city better than the country is that in the city everything is geared to working, and in the country everything is geared to relaxation. I like working better than relaxing. In the city, even the trees in the parks work hard because the number of people they have to make oxygen and chlorophyll for is staggering. If you lived in Canada you might have a million trees making oxygen for you alone, so each of those trees isn't working that hard. Whereas a tree in a treepot in Times Square has to make oxygen for a million people. In New York you really do have to hustle, and the trees know this, too – just look at them. The other day on 57th Street, I was walking and I was looking at the new, sloping Solow building across the street and I walked straight into a treepot. I was embarrassed because there was no way at all to carry it off. I just fell on top of this tree on West 57th Street because I wasn't ready for it to be there.

Somehow, the way life works, people usually wind up either in crowded subways and elevators, or in big rooms all by themselves. Everybody should have a big room they can go to and everybody should also ride the crowded subways.

Usually people are very tired when they ride on a subway, so they can't sing and dance, but I think if they could sing and dance on a subway, they'd really enjoy it.

The kids who spray graffiti all over the subway cars at night have learned how to recycle city space very well. They go back into the subway yards in the middle of the night when the cars are empty and that's when they do their singing and their dancing on the subway. The subways are like palaces at night with all that space just for you.

Ghetto space is wrong for America. It's wrong for people who are the same type to go and live together. There shouldn't be any huddling together in the same groups with the same food. In America it's got to mix 'n' mingle. If I were President, I'd make people mix 'n' mingle more. But the thing is America's a free country and I couldn't make them.

I believe in living in one room. One empty room with just a bed, a tray, and a suitcase. You can do everything either from your bed or in your bed – eat, sleep, think, get exercise, smoke – and you would have a bathroom and a telephone right next to the bed.

Everything is more glamorous when you do it in bed, anyway. Even peeling potatoes.

★

Suitcase space is so efficient. A suitcase full of everything you need:

> One spoon
> One fork
> One plate
> One cup
>
> One shirt
> One underwear
> One sock
> One shoe

One suitcase and one empty room. Terrific. Perfect.

By living in one room you eliminate a lot of worries. But the basic worries, unfortunately, remain:

> Are the lights on or off?
> Is the water off?
> Are the cigarettes out?
> Is the back door closed?
> Is the elevator working?
> Is there anyone in the lobby?
> Who's that sitting in my lap?

People are sleeping in pyramid-shaped spaces a lot now because they think it will keep them young and vital and stop the aging process. I'm not worried about that because I have my wings. However, my ideal too is the pyramid-look, because you don't have to think about a ceiling. You want to have a roof over your head, so why not let your walls also be your ceiling, so you have one less thing to think about – one less surface to look at, one less surface to clean, one less surface to paint. The tepee-dwelling Indians had the right idea. A cone might be nice if circles didn't exclude the edges and if you could find the right round sink, but I prefer an equilateral-triangular pyramidal-shaped enclosure even more than a square-based pyramid shape, because with a triangular base you have one less wall to think about, and one less corner to dust.

My ideal city would be one long Main Street with no cross streets or side streets to jam up traffic. Just one long oneway street. With one tall vertical building where everybody lived with:

> One elevator
> One doorman
> One mailbox
> One washing machine
> One garbage can
> One tree out front
> One movie theater next door

Main Street would be very very wide, and all you'd have to say to someone to make them feel good is, 'I saw you on Main Street today.'

And you'd fill your car up with gas and drive across the street.

My ideal city would be completely new. *No antiques.* All the buildings would be new. Old buildings are un-natural spaces. Buildings should be built to last for a short time. And if they're older than ten years, I say get rid of them. I'd build new buildings every fourteen years. The building and the tearing down would keep people busy, and the water wouldn't be rusty from old pipes.

Rome, Italy, is an example of what happens when the buildings in a city last too long.

They call Rome 'The Eternal City' because everything is so old and everything is still standing. They always say, 'Rome wasn't built in a day.' Well, I say maybe it should have been, because the quicker you build something, the shorter a time it lasts, and the shorter a time it lasts, the sooner people have jobs again, replacing it. Replacing necessities keeps people busy. The necessities, they always say, are food, shelter, and clothing. Now, in Italy they make a lot of food, and they make a lot of clothing, but food and clothing are only two-thirds of the necessities, the other third is shelter – and they're not making that because it's already been made. So what's happened in Rome is that the women wind up in the kitchens making all the food and in the factories sewing all the clothes, while the men don't do anything because the buildings are already built and they're not falling down! Their buildings were originally built too well and they've never corrected the situation. This is why you see so many men on the streets of Rome, Italy, at all hours of the day and night.

★

The best, most temporal way of making a building that I ever heard of is by making it with light. The Fascists did a lot of this 'light architecture.' If you build buildings with lights outside, you can make them indefinite, and then when you're through using them you shut the lights off and they disappear. Hitler always needed buildings in a hurry to make speeches from, so his architect created these 'buildings' for him that were illusion buildings, completely constructed by lighting effects, where he defined a very big space.

Holograms are going to be exciting, I think. You can really, finally, with holograms, pick your own atmosphere. They'll be televising a party, and you want to be there, and with holograms, you will be there. You'll be able to have this 3-D party in your house, you'll be able to pretend you're there and walk in with the people. You can even rent a party. You can have anybody famous that you want sitting right next to you.

I like to be the right thing in the wrong space and the wrong thing in the right space. But when you hit one of the two, people turn the lights out on you, or spit on you, or write bad reviews of you, or beat you up, or mug you, or say you're 'climbing.' But usually being the right thing in the wrong space and the wrong thing in the right space is worth it, because something funny always happens. Believe me, because I've made a career out of being the right thing in the wrong space and the wrong thing in the right space. That's one thing I really do know about.

When people have a cool, calm atmosphere about them, they're usually spaced. They have those right kind of eyes, and they sit around and not bother anybody. Some people are like that naturally because of their chemicals, and other people are like that because of drugs. They think they're thinking – about something.

Energy helps you fill up more space, but if I had more energy than usual, I'd probably not want to fill up more space – I'd be in my room cleaning a lot. I'll say this for diet pills: they make you think small, and when you think small, you do a lot of cleaning up. Real energy makes you want to run down the beach doing cartwheels even if you can't do them. But diet-pill energy helps you fill up less space because it makes you want to recopy address books while you *talk* for an hour about running down the beach doing cartwheels. Diet pills make you want to dust and flush things down the john.

In New York you have to clean so much, and when you're finished, it's not-dirty. In Europe people clean so much, and when they're finished, it's not just not-dirty, it's clean. Also, it seems so much easier to entertain in Europe than in New York. You just throw open the doors to the garden and eat out in the open air with flowers and trees all around. Whereas New York is funny, most of the time things just don't come off. In Europe, even having tea in the back yard can be wonderful. But in New York it's complicated – if the restaurant is nice, the food can be bad and if the food is good, the lighting can be bad, and if the lighting is good, the air circulation can be bad.

And New York restaurants now have a new thing – they don't sell their food, they sell their atmosphere. They say, 'How dare you say we don't have good food, when we never said we had good food. We have good *atmosphere*.' They caught on that what people really care about is changing their atmosphere for a couple of hours. That's why they can get away with just selling their atmosphere with a minimum of actual food. Pretty soon when food prices go really up, they'll be selling only atmosphere. If people are really all that hungry, they can bring food with them when they go out to dinner, but otherwise, instead of 'going out to dinner' they'll just be 'going out to atmosphere.'

My favorite restaurant atmosphere has always been the atmosphere of the good, plain, American lunchroom or even the good plain American lunchcounter. The old-style Schrafft's and the old-style Chock Full O' Nuts are absolutely the only things in the world that I'm truly nostalgic for. The days were carefree in the 1940s and 1950s when I could go into a Chocks for my cream cheese sandwich with nuts on date-nut bread and not worry about a thing. No matter what changes or how fast, the one thing we all always need is real good food so we can know what the changes are and how fast they're coming. Progress is very important and exciting in everything except food.

When you say you want an orange, you don't want someone asking you, 'An orange what?'

I really like to eat alone. I want to start a chain of restaurants for other people who are like me called ANDYMATS – 'The Restaurant for the Lonely Person.' You get your food and then you take your tray into a booth and watch television.

Today my favorite kind of atmosphere is the airport atmosphere. If I didn't have to think about the idea that airplanes go up in the air and fly it would be my perfect atmosphere. Airplanes and airports have my favorite kind of food service, my favorite kind of bathrooms, my favorite peppermint Life Savers, my favorite kinds of entertainment, my favorite loudspeaker address systems, my favorite conveyor belts, my favorite graphics and colors, the best security checks, the best views, the best perfume shops, the best employees, and the best optimism. I love the way you don't have to think about where you're going, someone else is doing that, but I just can't get over the crazy feeling I get when I look out and see the clouds and know I'm really up-there. The atmosphere is great, it's the idea of flying that I question. I guess I'm not an air person, but I'm on an air schedule, so I have to live an air life. I'm embarrassed that I don't like to fly because I love to be modern, but I compensate by loving airports and airplanes so much.

The best atmosphere I can think of is film, because it's three-dimensional physically and two-dimensional emotionally.

H. G. Wells *The Time Machine*
M. R. James *The Stalls of Barchester Cathedral*
Jane Austen *The History of England by a Partial, Prejudiced and Ignorant Historian*
Edgar Allan Poe *Hop-Frog*
Virginia Woolf *The New Dress*
Antoine de Saint-Exupéry *Night Flight*
Oscar Wilde *A Poet Can Survive Everything But a Misprint*
George Orwell *Can Socialists be Happy?*
Dorothy Parker *Horsie*
D. H. Lawrence *Odour of Chrysanthemums*
Homer *The Wrath of Achilles*
Emily Brontë *No Coward Soul Is Mine*
Romain Gary *Lady L.*
Charles Dickens *The Chimes*
Dante *Hell*
Georges Simenon *Stan the Killer*
F. Scott Fitzgerald *The Rich Boy*
Katherine Mansfield *A Dill Pickle*
Fyodor Dostoyevsky *The Dream of a Ridiculous Man*

Franz Kafka *A Hunger-Artist*

Leo Tolstoy *Family Happiness*

Karen Blixen *The Dreaming Child*

Federico García Lorca *Cicada!*

Vladimir Nabokov *Revenge*

Albert Camus *A Short Guide to Towns Without a Past*

Muriel Spark *The Driver's Seat*

Carson McCullers *Reflections in a Golden Eye*

Wu Cheng'en *Monkey King Makes Havoc in Heaven*

Friedrich Nietzsche *Ecce Homo*

Laurie Lee *A Moment of War*

Roald Dahl *Lamb to the Slaughter*

Frank O'Connor *The Genius*

James Baldwin *The Fire Next Time*

Hermann Hesse *Strange News from Another Planet*

Gertrude Stein *Paris France*

Seneca *Why I am a Stoic*

Snorri Sturluson *The Prose Edda*

Elizabeth Gaskell *Lois the Witch*

Sei Shōnagon *A Lady in Kyoto*

Yasunari Kawabata *Thousand Cranes*

Jack Kerouac *Tristessa*

Arthur Schnitzler *A Confirmed Bachelor*

Chester Himes *All God's Chillun Got Pride*

Bram Stoker *The Burial of the Rats*
Czesław Miłosz *Rescue*
Hans Christian Andersen *The Emperor's New Clothes*
Bohumil Hrabal *Closely Watched Trains*
Italo Calvino *Under the Jaguar Sun*
Stanislaw Lem *The Seventh Voyage*
Shirley Jackson *The Daemon Lover*
Stefan Zweig *Chess*
Kate Chopin *The Story of an Hour*
Allen Ginsberg *Sunflower Sutra*
Rabindranath Tagore *The Broken Nest*
Søren Kierkegaard *The Seducer's Diary*
Mary Shelley *Transformation*
Nikolai Leskov *Night Owls*
Willa Cather *A Lost Lady*
Emilia Pardo Bazán *The Lady Bandit*
W. B. Yeats *Sailing to Byzantium*
Margaret Cavendish *The Blazing World*
Lafcadio Hearn *Some Japanese Ghosts*
Sarah Orne Jewett *The Country of the Pointed Firs*
Vincent van Gogh *For Art and for Life*
Dylan Thomas *Do Not Go Gentle Into That Good Night*
Mikhail Bulgakov *A Dog's Heart*
Saadat Hasan Manto *The Price of Freedom*

Gérard de Nerval *October Nights*
Rumi *Where Everything is Music*
H. P. Lovecraft *The Shadow Out of Time*
Christina Rossetti *To Read and Dream*
Dambudzo Marechera *The House of Hunger*
Andy Warhol *Beauty*
Maurice Leblanc *The Escape of Arsène Lupin*
Eileen Chang *Jasmine Tea*
Irmgard Keun *After Midnight*
Walter Benjamin *Unpacking My Library*
Epictetus *Whatever is Rational is Tolerable*
Ota Pavel *How I Came to Know Fish*
César Aira *An Episode in the Life of a Landscape Painter*
Hafez *I am a Bird from Paradise*
Clarice Lispector *The Burned Sinner
and the Harmonious Angels*
Maryse Condé *Tales from the Heart*
Audre Lorde *Coal*
Mary Gaitskill *Secretary*
Tove Ditlevsen *The Umbrella*
June Jordan *Passion*
Antonio Tabucchi *Requiem*
Alexander Lernet-Holenia *Baron Bagge*
Wang Xiaobo *The Maverick Pig*